VOICES

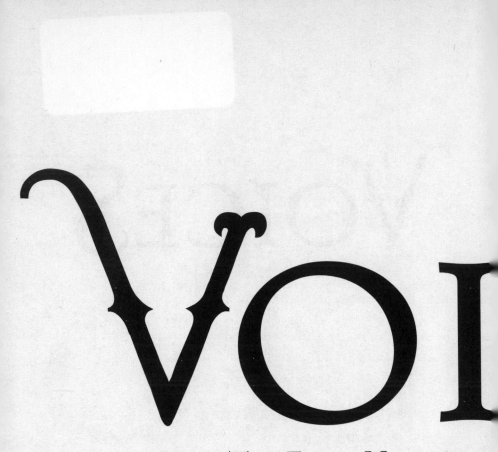

VOI

❖ THE FINAL HOURS

CES
OF JOAN OF ARC ❧

By DAVID ELLIOTT

Houghton Mifflin Harcourt
Boston New York

hmhbooks.com

The text was set in Adobe Jenson Pro.
Map art by Cara Llewellyn
Book design by Sharismar Rodriguez

The Library of Congress has cataloged the hardcover edition as follows:
Names: Elliott, David, 1947- author. | Title: Voices / by David Elliott.
Description: Boston : Houghton Mifflin Harcourt, [2019] Audience:
Grades 9–12. | Audience: Ages 14 and up.
Identifiers: LCCN 2018025855
Subjects: LCSH: Joan, of Arc, Saint, 1412–1431—Juvenile literature.
| Christian women saints—France—Biography—Juvenile literature. |
Christian saints—France—Biography—Juvenile literature. | Women
soldiers—France—Biography—Juvenile literature. | Soldiers—
France—Biography—Juvenile literature.
Classification: LCC DC103.5 .E45 2019 | DDC 944/.026092 [B]—
dc23
LC record available at https://lccn.loc.gov/2018025855

ISBN: 978-1-328-98759-4 hardcover
ISBN: 978-0-358-45208-9 paperback

Manufactured in the United States of America
DOC 10 9 8 7 6 5 4 3 2 1
4500817706

To Kate O'Sullivan, editor extraordinaire
and Kelly Sonnack, agent nonpareil—
women warriors in their own right.
How lucky I am!

BEFORE YOU READ

Much of what we know about Joan of Arc comes from the transcripts of her two trials. The first, the Trial of Condemnation, convened in 1431, found Joan guilty of "relapsed heresy" and famously burned her at the stake. The second, the Trial of Nullification, held some twenty-four years after her death, effectively revoked the findings of the first. In both cases, the politics of the Middle Ages guaranteed their outcomes before they started. It is in the Trial of Condemnation that we hear Joan in her own voice answering the many questions her accusers put to her. In the Trial of Nullification, her relatives, childhood friends, and comrades-in-arms bear witness to the girl they knew. Throughout *Voices*, you will find direct quotes from these trials.

Oh, one more thing: Because the book is written in rhymed and metered verse, it's important to get the pronunciation of the French names and places right. Here's a quick pronunciation guide to help you out.

DOMRÉMY: dom-ray-MI (very much like the song)

TROYES: twah (rhymes more or less with "law")

CHINON: she-NOHN

VAUCOULEURS: voh-koo-LEUHR

ORLÉANS: OR-lee-OHN (three, not two, syllables)

PATAY: puh-TYE

REIMS: rahnce (not reems)

ROUEN: ROO-uhn (kind of like the English word "ruin")

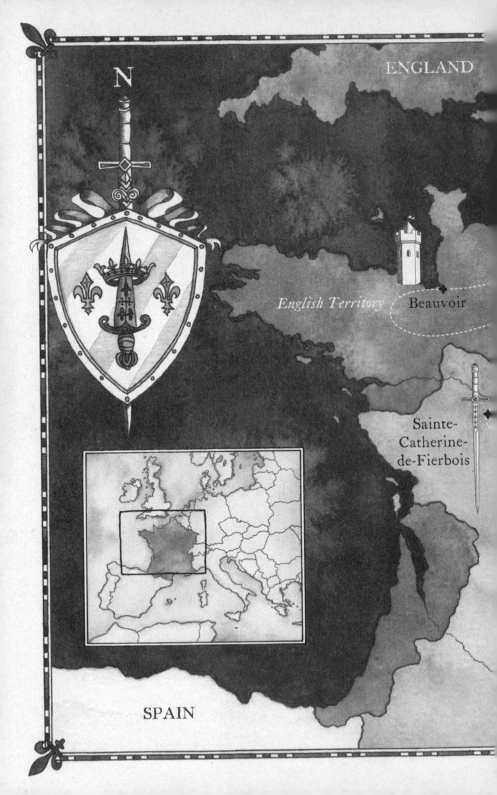

ENGLAND

English Territory

Beauvoir

Sainte-
Catherine-
de-Fierbois

SPAIN

✢ PROLOGUE ✢

ROM *her earliest years till her departure,*
Jeannette [Joan] the Maid was a good girl, chaste,
simple, modest, never blaspheming God nor the
Saints, fearing God. . . . Often she went with her
sister and others to the Church and Hermitage of
Bermont.

> Perrin Le Drapier, churchwarden and
> bell-ringer of the Parish Church
> Trial of Nullification

THE CANDLE

I
recall
it as if it were
yesterday. She was
so lovely and young. In
her hand I darted and flick-
ered away, an ardent lover's ad-
venturing tongue. I had never known
such yearning, exciting and risky and
cruel. As we walked to the church, I was
burning; she was my darling, my future,
my fuel. I wanted to set her afire right then.
But she was so pure, so chaste; her innocence
only increased my desire. Still, I know the
dangers of haste. So I watched and I studied
and waited, and I saw that her young blood
ran hot. She had no idea we were fated. I
could name what she craved; she could
not. Then in her eye, I caught my
reflection. In her eye, I saw myself shine, and I saw the heat
rise on her virgin's com-
plexion. That's when
I knew: She was
mine.

VOICES

❖ THE FINAL HOURS OF JOAN OF ARC ❖

JOAN

I've heard it said that when we die
the soul discards its useless shell,
and our life will flash before our
eyes. Is this a gift from Heaven?
Or a jinx from deepest Hell? Only
the dying know, but what the dying
know the dying do not tell. What
more the dying know it seems I
am about to learn. For when the
sun is at its highest, a lusting torch
will touch the pyre. The flames will rise.
And I will burn. But I have always
been afire. With youth. With faith. With
truth. And with desire. My name is
Joan, but I am called the Maid. My
hands are bound behind me. The fire
beneath me laid.

FIRE

I yearn I yearn I yearn my darling
I yearn I yearn I yearn

JOAN

Every life is its own story—
not without a share of glory,
and not without a share of grief.
I lived like a hero at seventeen.
At nineteen, I die like a thief.

I'll begin with my family:
a father, a mother, uncles
and aunts, one sister, two brothers,
all born in Lorraine in the
Duchy of Bar. Domrémy is
our village. It's north of the Loire,
the chevron-shaped river that cuts
across France. My parents were peasants,
caught up in the dance that all the
oppressed must step to and master:
work harder, jump higher, bow lower,
run faster. The feel of the earth
beneath my bare feet, the sun on
my face, the smell of the wheat as
it breaks through the soil, the curve of
the sprout as it bends and uncoils,

the song of the beetle, the hum
of the bees. I was comforted
by these, but they would not have
satisfied me, for something other
occupied me. To take the path
that I have taken, I have abandoned
and forsaken everything I
once held dear, and that, in part, has
brought me here, to die alone bound
to this stake. Each decision that
we make comes with a hidden price.
We're never told what it is we
may be asked to sacrifice.

A shape begins to form itself
in the air in front of me. Trunk . . .
and roots . . . an ancient tree, its limbs
so low they touch the earth. I know
it now. Around its girth we village
children sang and danced. The tree was
thought to be entranced; our elders
said beneath its shade a band of

brownies lived and played. I wonder
if they live there still, or have, like
me, they been betrayed?

NOT *far from Domrémy there is a tree that they called "The Ladies Tree"—others call it "The Fairies Tree." . . . Often I have heard the old folk—they are not of my lineage—say that the fairies haunt this tree. . . . I have seen the young girls putting garlands on the branches of this tree, and I myself have sometimes put them there with my companions.*

Joan
Trial of Condemnation

THE FAIRY TREE

I sing the mournful carol of five hundred passing years. Nurtured by the howling wind and the music of the spheres, I have retained the record of every heart that ever broke, every wound that ever bled. I remember single drops of rain, every day of golden light, the sorrow of the cuckoo's crimes, the lightning strikes, the trill of every lark. And I have stored the memory of these consecrated things in the scarred and winding surface of my incandescent bark. Etched there, too? The face of every child who cherished me, who sang my name—the Fairy Tree. They came to celebrate the sprites who lived beneath my canopy, for I was the fairies' chosen, their sylvan hideaway. The brindled cows looked on at human folly when the fairies were charged and banished by the village priest. The children, too, have vanished, undone by years, and worms, and melancholy. Yes, all my children I recall, but it is Joan who of them all stands apart in the concentric circles of my ringèd memory. She hid it well—the burning coal that was her heart. But a tree is ever watchful in the presence of a flame, and I saw in her a smoldering, a spark, a heat well beyond extinguishing. I feel it even now, that heat. It blazes just the same. Elements not reconciled, as disparate as day and night, sparked an unrelenting friction destined to ignite something hybrid, new, and wild. It was a heavy fate for such a child, so small and young. And yet among the girls she was a favorite, their affection for her zealous. But the boys were threatened. Rough. Rugged. Strong. Athletic. They did not know that they were jealous. I see now it was prophetic, the rancor hidden in their hearts. But rancor is a stubborn guest; once lodged, it won't depart. The village priest abides here still, or his likely twin, still finding evil in every joy, still scolding the girls, still eyeing the boys, still holding up pleasure and calling it sin. As for the girl, for Joan, she remains a mystery. Who can say why some arrive and then depart forgotten while others fashion history?

JOAN

The illusion of the tree is
fading. I see my mother now,
separating good peas from the
bad. Clad in homespun, she has just
come from the stable. But the light
is dim. I am unable to
see her careworn face, and so I
trace the swift movement of her hands—
the blunt fingers callused and bent,
the rough knuckles swollen and cracked.
But those earthly imperfections
could never detract from the inborn
grace with which they move, the rough
gestures that I know and love. When
I left Domrémy to join the
world of soldiery and men, how
could I have known that I would
never feel my mother's touch or
see her hands again?

EANNE [*Joan*] *was born at Domrémy and was baptized at the Parish Church of Saint Remy, in that place. Her father was named Jacques d'Arc, her mother Isabelle—both laborers living together at Domrémy. They were, as I saw and knew, good and faithful Catholics, laborers of good repute and honest life.*

Jean Morel, laborer
Trial of Nullification

ISABELLE

What is a *woman?*
Her brothers' sister, her father's *daughter,*
Her husband's wife, her children's *mother.*
Milk the cow, churn the butter, slop the pig, *spin*
the flax, nurse the sick, boil the soup, *knead*
the dough, bake the bread, *mind*

the children, mind the sheep, *mind*
your manners. These are what a *woman*
learns to become a wife, skills all women *need,*
and skills I have passed on to Joan, my *daughter.*
I taught her to churn, to bake, to plant, to *spin.*
Wasn't that my duty as her *mother?*

I learned them as a girl from my own *mother,*
who learned them as a girl from hers. *Mind*
you, there are days my head *spins*
like the stars over me, but a *woman*
is not her own master. She is the *daughter*
of Urgency, a servant to *Need.*

From the start, Joan didn't *need*
or want what other girls needed, her *mother,*
for example. It hurts to have a *daughter*

who so clearly knows her own *mind*.
Such qualities are dangerous in a *woman*.
She was a contradiction, able to sew and *spin*

better than any girl in the village, married or *spin-*
ster. And what she could do with a *need-*
le, well, there is still not a *woman*
who could match her. But a *mother?*
A farmer's wife? No. In my *mind*
she was more son than *daughter,*

keeping her silence, a *daughter*
who would churn, cook, sew, *spin*
without complaint. Yet her *mind*
was elsewhere, settled on another *need,*
a need she could not share with her *mother*
or any other *woman*.

Mothers should understand what their *daughters*
need. But Joan and I were never of one *mind*.
Spin! I begged her. Spin like a *woman!*

JOAN

To spin like a woman was not
my fate. I had other talents,
concealed but innate, that even
now are hard for me to comprehend.
I only know that to wash and
mend my brothers' tunics aroused
in me an aching discontent.
This low unhappiness was the
advent of everything that followed. But
I swallowed my pride, nodded, smiled,
and swore that I would best every
female task my mother assigned. All
that to which I felt more naturally
inclined I vowed to put aside.
But the harder I tried, the more
it pressed. I was beset by my
own nature, possessed by a ruthless
and persistent urge, as if there
were another me waiting to
emerge from all that was constraining.
But about this, I said nothing
and continued with my training.

N your youth, did you learn any trade?"

Joan: *"Yes, I learnt to spin and to sew; in sewing and spinning I fear no woman in Rouen."*

Trial of Condemnation

THE NEEDLE

In
the circle of
women is where I am
found, stitching and hem-
ming and   mending.

Pulled by   fingers hard-
skinned,   roughened,
and browned,   in the circle
of women is   where I am
found; we   labor in
silence, no   song and no
sound, the   drudge of it
never ending.   In the circle of
women is   where I am
found, stitch-   ing and hem-
ming and   mending. I've
been handled   by many, both
maiden and   crone, the
clumsy as well   as the skilled,
the artful, the   novice, the dull-
ard, the drone.   I've been handled by many,   both maiden
and crone, but   no one could
touch her, the   girl they called
Joan. Fero-   cious, focused,
strong-willed.   I've been handled by many,   both maiden
and crone, the   clumsy as well
as the skilled.   She was a
warrior, the   linen her foe,
and I was her   weapon, her
sword. How   quickly we
conquered!   How fast we
would go!   She was a
warrior, the   linen her foe.
The pace was   unyielding
and thrilling,   but oh! the
source of   conflict remained unexplored. She was a
warrior, the linen her foe, and
I was her weapon, her sword.

JOAN

France was then engaged, as now, in
a bitter civil war, a conflict
that had raged since long before I
became my parents' daughter. Contest
after contest, slaughter after slaughter
because of one woman's monstrous
treachery. Isabeau, our queen,
famed for her lechery, had signed
a treaty in the city of
Troyes. With no regard for custom
or law, she turned her back on her
own son. The English king, Henry,
would now be the one to ascend
the French throne, not Charles VII,
blood of her blood and bone of her
bone. Some of my countrymen were
slyly misled. When Isabeau
spoke, they nodded their heads and
meekly agreed. They now fight for
Henry, an English weed taking
up space where he never belonged.
But *I* was for Charles, wronged by
his mother. *He* was my king.
Charles! No other!

The English were hated by the
true French. We hated their language,
their manners, their stench when it
tainted our air the day they
invaded. Henry had even
taken the city of Paris,
while our gentle dauphin, shaken
and harassed, headed south of the
Loire, where he had strong support. In
the town of Chinon, he established
his court.

I wanted to fight! I wanted to
go! But I was made to sit and
sew while Henry overran our home,
a savage, deadly pestilence.
My energy, my passion, even
my intelligence were forced into
an ever-smaller and suffocating
space. I felt smothered and entombed
in the coffin of the commonplace.

I longed to join the men in the
din and heat of battle.

But even my father's cattle
had more freedom. While my brothers
went to war, I sewed and burned with
rage. My dress was a red silence,
a hemmed and homespun cage.

EANNE *was older than I. I knew her and remember her for the three or four years before her departure from home. She was a well brought up girl, and well behaved.*

Dominique Jacob, childhood aquaintance
Trial of Nullification

SILENCE

I am blood
that's never bled.
I am Saturn.
I am lead,
both mineral
and malice.

I am prayer
that's never heard,
folded wings,
a captive bird,
the poison
in the chalice.

A hymn,
a dirge
that's never sung,
a pregnant doe
that's shot and hung,
contagion
in the palace.

The starving babe
that never cried,
the wish unheard,
the dream denied,
the heart that formed
a callus.

JOAN

Now the village church appears, my
beloved Saint Remy, where every
afternoon I went to pray. On
its stone and well-swept floor I knelt
and begged for clarity. And there,
I often met the gaunt, forgotten
poor. Victims of the plague and the
English war, they wandered, starving,
without roof or bed. Too soon they
would be living with the dead, a
sparse and rotting banquet for the
hungry worms and biting flies. I
gave them what I could, a coin, a
crust of bread. I forced myself to
look into their eyes and wondered
how a just and loving God could
allow these blameless lives to be
so sorrow-filled and flawed.
I'll learn the answer to this question
soon. The sun is rising. And with it
noon.

FIRE

I burn I burn I burn my darling
I burn I burn I burn
I yearn I yearn I yearn my darling
I yearn I yearn I yearn

MY father's house joined the house of Jacques d'Arc so I knew her well. We often spun together, and together worked at the ordinary house-duties, whether by day or night. She was a good Christian, of good manners and well brought up. She loved the Church, and went there often, and gave alms.

Mengette
Trial of Nullification

ALMS

I am a nomad.
I am called Alms.
I pass from hand to hand,
from palm to outstretched
palm. Like sand battered
on a storm-tossed strand,
I am unsettled and un-
planned. Unquiet
and uncalm.

What I seek
I cannot find: a place
to rest. My happiness ever
undermined. How cruel a
jest that I myself have been
oppressed by the shiftless
dispossessed, the chaff
of humankind.

But in her lov-
ing hand I was content.
I cannot understand. Was
it just an accident? What did
my restlessness invent? Some
say that she was Heaven
sent: here by God's
command.

I travel still, but
I retain the peace I
found when in her charge.
My pain released, allayed,
unbound, the change she
wrought in me profound,
as if I had been blighted
ground, and she
was rain.

JOAN

It is hard to see my childhood
replayed before me like a dream.
Now I see the Meuse, the village
stream where I so often led my
father's team of oxen. How I
miss those cool and softly sloping
banks. And near it graze the gentle
brutes themselves, steam rising from their
backs and muscled flanks.

ID *you not take the animals to the fields?"*

Joan: *"When I was bigger and had come to years of discretion, I did not look after them generally; but I helped take them to the meadows."*

Trial of Condemnation

THE CATTLE

What did she hear that we did not?
What was that faraway look in her eye?
The unthinking step, the mournful sigh,
this girl unstudied and untaught,

trapped as if she'd been caged and caught
like a fledgling lark that is longing to fly.
What did she hear that we did not?
What was that faraway look in her eye?

Was it love, with its tender, unknowable knot,
or madness chanting its lullaby
out in the meadow beneath the blue sky?
Was she enraptured? Or was she distraught?
What did she hear that we did not?

JOAN

What was it that I saw and heard?
In the beginning was the word,
the word that I am bound to now
as much as to this rigid stake.
They counseled me to disavow,
to say that I was not awake.
But only I know what occurred.
In the beginning was the word.

I was thinning the young seedlings,
an ordinary morning, when
abruptly, without sound,
without a moment's warning, the
world filled with a dazzling and
celestial light. I thought my time
on earth was done and struggled to
recite a final holy prayer.
My hands went to my eyes, which were
blinded by the glare when all the
world around me blazed and disappeared.
And then, as if he'd been there always,
holy, fierce, majestic, and revered,
Saint Michael, the Archangel, broke
through the sacred luminescence.

In his uncorrupted presence,
other angels, six of them or
seven, each one descended from
the brilliant heights of Heaven. It
was as if I had awakened
from a profound and binding trance.
All life, birds, brutes, even the ants
knelt and bowed their horned and sharp-jawed
heads, and the spiders hanging from
their fine and silver threads stopped their
endless industry to hear what
the blessèd angel said, the air
around him spiced with the cologne
of countless flowers. And I don't
know if I stood there for some
minutes or for hours, when in a
voice that seemed to pierce the very
fabric of the air, he spoke to
me as I stood trembling, weeping
there. "Be good," he said. "Be good." I
was awash in fear but somehow
I understood that if I kept
this holy caution I would play
a leading role in a sacred

strategy, which at some future
time would be revealed to me, and
that everything about my life
had been anticipated and foreseen.
I was very young then, just thirteen.

HAT *was the first voice that came to you?"*

Joan: *"It was Saint Michael: I saw him before my eyes; he was not alone, but quite surrounded by the Angels of Heaven."*

"Did you see Saint Michael and these angels bodily and in reality?"

Joan: *"I saw them with my bodily eyes as well as I see you."*

Trial of Condemnation

♋ SAINT MICHAEL ♋

They say I'm a saint. But are there such things?
And an archangel, too, apparently.
In every painting, I'm there, with wings,
all frill and froth and feathery,
a halo set behind me,
like a shining china platter
on the long and sagging table of a grand marquis.
But in the end, what does it matter?

The harp and that halo, all those things
that call forth your pale notion of divinity—
the choir that so often and so loudly sings!—
the trappings of a profligate reality?
Or the set piece of an ostentatious fantasy?
Some propose the former; others claim the latter,
depending on their mood or their theology.
But in the end, what does it matter?

From the guileless peasant to the cunning king,
all have speculated on what I might be.
What hilarious suppositions! What fabulous
    imaginings!

And what a tragic lack of creativity.
"Saint" Peggy and "Saint" Cate agree;
it couldn't make us sadder.
Odd, for such a comedy.
But in the end, what does it matter?

What did the girl hear? What did she see?
The product of a septic mind and its deceitful
chatter?
Or did I actually appear? *Is there actually a me?*

My friends, what does it matter?

JOAN

He often came to see me after
that. And never alone. Saint Margaret
and Saint Catherine sat on either
side. Each on a golden throne. The
saints were very kind to me and
spoke often of a prophecy,
which from ancient times foretold
that a woman, shameless, bold,
would be the country's ruination
and that its only true salvation
lay with a virgin from Lorraine.
Their countenances made it plain
who these two were meant to be. The
first was heartless Isabeau, the
next, they said, was *me*. They said that
all had been decided. France would
no longer be divided; that
humble though my circumstance, I
would defend and rescue France. They
spoke to me in lilting voices, sweet as
the song of birds.

Some will hear these words and think me
ill, a victim of delusion.

Some will say the Devil's fiendish
fancy is the source of my confusion
and will seek out explanations
that fit within the comfort of
their own imaginations. But I
have learned that life is more complex,
that the door between this world and
the next is sometimes left ajar,
and that each of us is more, far
more, than we are told we are.

HIS *Voice that speaks to you, is it that of an Angel, or of a Saint, or from God direct?"*

Joan: *"It is the Voice of Saint Catherine and of Saint Margaret. Their faces are adorned with beautiful crowns, very rich and precious."*

Trial of Condemnation

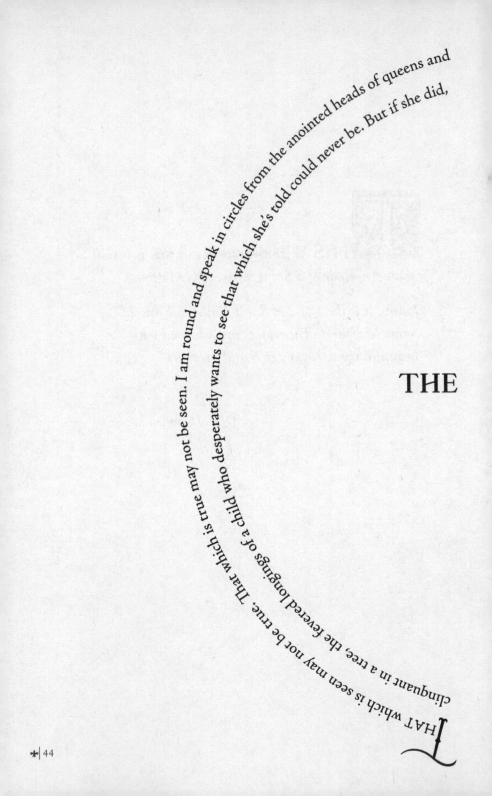

THE

HAT which is seen may not be true. That which is true may not be seen. I am round and speak in circles from the anointed heads of queens and clinquant in a tree, the fevered longings of a child who desperately wants to see that which she's told could never be. But if she did, possible or would-be saints and fat and craven kings. I can be made of many things: thorns woven into diadems, gold and silver, precious gems, sunlight or morning dew? That which is seen may not be true. Pearls or diamonds? That which is true may not be seen. I can be made of many things: what might it mean?

CROWN

JOAN

In those confounding early days
I was badly shaken. I had
been taken from one world into
another, as if I were no
more than a feather, tossed and blown
by a compelling wind. As I
churned the cream or thinned the seedlings
in the garden, I began to
feel as if I were on loan to
my parents or that my life in
Domrémy was only a dream
from which I would one day be roused.
I went about my daily obligations,
and waited for the holy visitations,
which began to come more frequently.
I marveled at the change that was
happening in me, for just the
way the darkened world is brightened
after it has stormed, my soul was
filled with divine light, my discontent
transformed.

But then my father said my time
had come to marry. There was no

question: I refused. This unsettled
and confused him. It was the first
time I had balked at his authority.
When he felt his tight, paternal
grip loosening on me, his manner
quickly changed from indifferent to
grim, but my allegiance now was
to myself, not to another
man, and especially not to him.

DID *not your father have dreams about you before your departure?"*

Joan: *"When I was still with my father and mother, my mother told me many times that my father had spoken of having dreamed that I, Joan, his daughter, went away with men-at-arms. My father and mother took great care to keep me safe, and held me much in subjection. I obeyed them in everything, except in the case in Toul—the action for marriage. I have heard my mother say that my father told my brothers, 'Truly, if I thought this thing would happen that I have dreamed about my daughter, I would wish you to drown her; and, if you would not do it, I would drown her myself.'"*

Trial of Condemnation

JACQUES D'ARC

I am a simple farmer, a plainspoken *man*,
hard-working and God-fearing, just as my *father*
before me. It was he who taught me to keep my *eye*
on the weather, my sheep, my wife and *daughter*.
And what he taught, I will teach my *sons*
and they will teach theirs, each season, each *life*,

each generation following the other. This is *life*
as it has been and will be until *man-*
kind is no more and the *sun's*
rays quit the fields. As a *father*
I fulfilled my duty to protect my *daughter*.
I taught her to keep her *eye*

turned inward, to reject temptation, to avoid the *eye*
of the serpent, unlike Eve, who traded *life*
in the Garden to know evil. Woman is the *daughter*
of sin, and if unchecked, the ruination of a good *man*,
the humiliation and sorrow of a loving *father*,
an embarrassment to her brothers and *sons*.

My wife has given me three fine *sons*.
Their backs are strong and straight; their *eyes*
are clear. They will honor me, their *father*,

when I take my place on the great circle of *life*.
I am a farmer, but am richer than a noble*man*
whose wife's womb yields only *daughters*.

And as for Joan, my eldest *daughter*,
she was stronger in temperament than my *sons*,
as grave in her demeanor as a virtuous *man*.
But I sometimes saw a spark in her *eye*:
the spark of ambition. It would ruin her *life*
and the name and reputation of her *father*.

Obedient, chaste, respectful to her mother and *father*,
in almost every way, she was the perfect *daughter*,
working more in a week than many girls do in a *life-*
time. But she would never bear me grand*sons*.
I knew this as sure as I knew that ox*eye*
daisies thrive over the grave of an honest *man*.

Daughter, I said to her. Listen to your *father*.
Man is your light. Find a husband. Give him *sons*.
Life wants nothing from you. Remove that spark
    from your *eye!*

JOAN

The morning sky is gray, and a
crowd begins to form. The townsfolk
are aroused today. Buzzing like
a swarm of bees, they have come to
watch me die. Some of them are ill
at ease, but not as ill at ease
as I. Reluctant to remember,
reluctant to forget, I am
defiant in my triumph but
taunted with regret. I think
of all I have experienced,
and all that I have not, everything I kept in darkness and the
suffering that it brought. I did not
tell my father that I would never
wed. I did not tell myself that
I had other desires instead,
desires that I fought against,
desires I could not name, desires
that spoke an unknown tongue, desires
that lit a flame. Even now when
at the end, with nothing left to
lose, I cannot identify
what I could never choose.

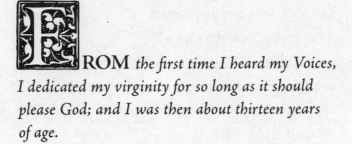ROM *the first time I heard my Voices, I dedicated my virginity for so long as it should please God; and I was then about thirteen years of age.*

Joan
Trial of Condemnation

VIRGINITY

I am a bed
forever made.
I am a fortress,
a stockade,
a desert and
a garden.

I am a chamber,
ever locked.
I am a weapon,
never cocked.
A sentence and
a pardon.

A stone,
a field
unsown,
unplowed,
a vow,
a habit,
gown
and shroud,
I soften and
I harden.

I am
an absence,
a tranquil
O.
I am all
she will
never know,

her prisoner
and her warden.

JOAN

The next three years I often spent
alone. I did my chores as always
but the angels had shown me that
my life was not what I thought that
it would be. I was sometimes then
in a state of ecstasy, marred
only by the anxiety
of knowing what I was called to
do. But as time passed, my confidence
slowly grew until the day my
saints instructed me to leave my
Domrémy for the nearby town
of Vaucouleurs, where Robert de
Baudricourt, my voices said, would
get me to Chinon and the unanointed
king. I left my family, my
friends, everything I had loved or
known. I did not say goodbye;
they would not have let me leave. I
was a girl. I was alone. There
was no other choice but to deceive.

HE *Voice said to me: ". . . Go, raise the siege which is being made before the city of Orléans. Go!" it added, "to Robert de Baudricourt." . . . I went to my uncle [Durand Laxart] and said that I wished to stay with him for a time. I remained there eight days. I said to him, "I must go to Vaucouleurs."*

Joan
Trial of Condemnation

THE ROAD TO VAUCOULEURS

I do not know where I begin.
And where I end I do not
know. I do not move but still
I bend. Was I a traitor or her
friend? What does her destiny
portend? I do not know.

Upon my back I felt her weight.
She walked alone upon my back.
She passed the fields, the mound-
ed stacks, the surest step I've ever
known and yet a girl not fully
grown upon my back.

I took her there. To her longed-
for destination I took her.
There was no choice. I took
her where she would begin her
new vocation. To her glory
and damnation, I took her there.

I do not know where I begin.
And where I end I do not know.
I do not move but still I bend.
Was I a traitor or her friend?
What does her destiny por-
tend? I do not know.

JOAN

I never once looked back.
From that bright morning to this
black day, there's been for me
no other way. In the fearless song
of every serenading bird,
I hear one pure and piercing anthem:
Onward!

WHEN *I arrived, I recognized Robert de Baudricourt, although I had never seen him. I knew him, thanks to my Voice, which made me recognize him. I said to Robert, "I must go into France!" [France was equivalent to wherever Charles was.] Twice Robert refused to hear me, and repulsed me. The third time, he received me, and furnished me with men.*

Joan
Trial of Condemnation

ROBERT DE BAUDRICOURT

It is a testimony to my iron *will*
that Vaucouleurs has never lost its *way*.
I have kept the English army *out*
because I am a man, the kind of *man*
who brooks no fools. I have no *time*
for prophets, seers, dupes who have a *dream*

and think it leads to truth. What is a *dream*
but a storehouse of a day's events? And who *will*
say it's more is he who wastes my *time*.
Or so I used to say, the narrow *way*
I used to think. Now I'm like a *man*
evicted from his home, who's been turned *out*

from the comfort of his own beliefs, *out-*
done and conquered by a girl who *dreamed*
that she and she alone would do what no *man*
has done, who came to me and said, "I *will*
expel from France all those who break *away*
from Charles, the rightful king, and the *time*

has come for you to help me in my quest." But *time*
was short, she said. She insisted she must go *out*
of Vaucouleurs, that I must help her find her *way*

to Charles, that I must help fulfill her *dream*,
that I, Robert, was subject to her *will*,
which was the holy will of God. What *man*

would dare to speak to me like this? What *man*
would have such insolence? Time after *time*
she came to me. A girl! But the power of her *will*
was stronger than my own. Twice, I threw her *out*
but dogged as a sharp, recurrent *dream*,
she reappeared, standing in my door*way*

like a boulder, in her off-putting *way*,
her shoulders squared, as bold as any *man*
I've ever known. Now I often day*dream*
about that uncanny girl. Though my *time*
in Vaucouleurs with her was brief, through*out*
my life, I've not met another like her. I never *will*.

In the end, I was a *man* in a dream, her *dream*,
and afflicted with the sentiment that my *time* was
    running *out*.
"Take what you need," I said. "I *will* not stand in
    your *way*."

JOAN

I endured the scorn of Baudricourt,
his contempt, his mocking laughter, and
the rank hostility of all
the men who came after. Though assailed
by their derision, I prevailed.
My vision never faltered. I
stood in front of them unafraid,
unaltered, until gradually
their privilege and their power
began to fade and weaken like
a flower in a time of drought.
If ever I was plagued by
anxiety or doubt, I put it
aside and fought arrogance with
arrogance and pride with
burnished pride.

FIRE

I thrill I thrill I thrill my darling
I thrill I thrill I thrill
I burn I burn I burn my darling
I burn I burn I burn
I yearn I yearn I yearn my darling
I yearn I yearn I yearn

JOAN

"Take what you need," he said. I stood
before him in my red dress and
made a list. I would need men to
give assistance and escort me,
men who would comport themselves
with honor, men I could trust, men
who could control their lust. For when
we traveled to Chinon, I would
have no female chaperone to
shield me from these knights and squires,
who might publicly admire my
valor and my spirit but privately
would prove themselves by trying to
get near it. The road, I knew, was
treacherous, our enemies
surrounding us until we crossed
the river Loire, our destination
far away. So I determined,
come what may, that I would not depart
unarmed. I would meet the future
king unharmed, untouched by guide or
English horde. My heart was pounding in
my side when I asked him for his sword.

ROM *Vaucouleurs, I departed . . . armed with a sword given me by Robert de Baudricourt, but without other arms.*

Joan
Trial of Condemnation

THE SWORD

I am a
sword, an instru-
ment of men, a blade
conceived in fire and
thrust in malice.
What did she
want with me,
this maid? I
am a sword!
An instrument
of men! A blade!
Attack! Defend!
Impale! Invade!
Penetrate!
Both tongue and
phallus, I am a
sword, an instru-
ment of men, a

blade conceived in fire and thrust in malice. Pommel. Cross-guard. Point and hilt. She held my
manly parts. She took them without shame or guilt—pommel, cross-guard, point, and hilt—as if she,
too, were forged

of steel; we were counterparts. Pommel. Cross-guard. Point and hilt. She held my manly parts. How firm her grip How strong her hand. She was as steady as a knight. Impossible to understand how firm her grip, how strong. Her hand a b l a z e with power, command, this girl so young and slight. How firm her grip. How strong her hand. She was as steady as a knight.

JOAN

But I knew a sword was not enough.
I would not meet my king in a
rough red dress, a signal that I
was less than I knew myself to
be. My blessed saints had given me
the liberty that I had always
craved, a freedom I had not been
brave enough to take. Now, at last,
I resolved that I would shake off
the russet shell that had defined
me, locked in, constrained, and
undermined me. The young dauphin
would find the Maid as she was truly
meant to be. Though I knew I would
be subject to every kind of
ridicule and personal attack,
I took a breath and crossed a line.
There would be no going back.

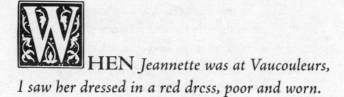

WHEN *Jeannette was at Vaucouleurs,*
I saw her dressed in a red dress, poor and worn.

Jean de Metz, squire
Trial of Nullification

THE RED DRESS

I can't forget that day
in Vaucouleurs. She tore me
from her body as if I'd stained
her skin, and left me like a
corpse on the cold, indurate floor.
She'd worn me every day—no
choice—but at her very core she bore
me an antipathy as sharp as any pin. No,
I won't forget that day in Vaucouleurs—
the way she turned and walked so boldly
out the door, leaving me to wonder, alone
with my chagrin, as lifeless as a corpse on a cold,
indurate floor. I'd never heard her laugh like that
before, as if she'd been relieved of agony that
twisted deep within. On that strange and fateful day
in Vaucouleurs, it was in that very room she knelt
and swore to never wear a woman's shift again.
Once she left me on that cold, indurate floor, she disappeared; I never saw her more. What was my transgression?
What my sin? Forgotten in the town of Vaucouleurs,
abandoned like a corpse on a cold, indurate floor.

JOAN

The dress was made of homespun that
I myself had cut and sewn, yet
it pressed against my shoulders as
cumbersome as stone. There were times
I had the strange idea it longed
to pull me down. But I would have
felt the same in any dress or
gown, even those constructed of
rich brocades and lace. In vestments
other women wear with ease, I
felt false and out of place. But that
day in Vaucouleurs I knew there
was attire that suited me much
better, clothing in which I saw
myself solid and unfettered,
and in which I would no longer
play the mute in an a dishonorable
charade. So I stepped out of the
red dress and left behind the
masquerade, the costume, and the
mask. And with it Joan the girl and
daughter, and her domestic tasks.

I ASKED *her when she wished to start. "Sooner at once than tomorrow, and sooner tomorrow than later," she said. I asked her also if she could make this journey dressed as she was. She replied she would willingly take a man's dress.*

Jean de Metz, squire
Trial of Nullification

THE TUNIC

I can't forget that day in Vaucouleurs
or how naturally I lay against her
breasts. From that day forward, nothing
was the same. We were a natural complement,
like sea and shore, or two parts of a
riddle heretofore un- guessed. I can't forget
that day in Vaucouleurs. When she wore me for
the first time, her happi- ness was pure; her joy was
unrepressed. From that day forward, nothing was the
same. The dress was like a costume. It forced her to
defer to strange, conflicting feelings that could never
be expressed. On that February day in Vaucouleurs,
she had a secret fever; she thought I was the cure. And
for a moment each of us was blessed. From that day
forward, nothing was the same. From that day forward, nothing was the same. From that day forward,
nothing was the same. From that day forward . . .

JOAN

I have led men into the nether-
world of battle. I have contended
to the tumult and the rattle
of besmirched and bloodied swords. I
have rallied screaming soldiers toward
their death, stepped over fallen warriors
to the rasp of their last breath. But
the boldest action I have
taken was in that domestic
dressing room. It led directly
to myself, and directly to
my doom. How often did they ask
me why I would not wear a dress.
How they frequently berated
me and urged me to confess that
to put on the clothes of men was
a foul abomination. They
said it was a mortal sin and
even promised me salvation
from the smoke and scorching fire if
I would just recant and put on
women's attire, the way, they said,
that God Himself intended. They
said my tunic and my doublet

derided and offended all
that to Him was sacred. And in
a moment of great weakness, I
recanted and relented. They
offered me a dress; I nodded and
consented and said that I would
wear it. But once back in my tower
cell, I knew I could not bear it–
the simple dress they proffered and
my own hypocrisy. I took
off the shift and donned the clothes more
natural to me. I knew then
I would face my death unafraid
and proud. If that meant that my
tunic would also be my shroud,
then I would enter Paradise
a bright and shining jewel, *not* an
abomination, but the way
that God has made me, His singular
creation.

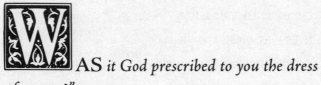 **W**AS *it God prescribed to you the dress of a man?"*

Joan: *"I did not take it by the advice of any man in the world. I did not take this dress or do anything but by the command of Our Lord and of the Angels."*

Trial of Condemnation

JOAN

How strange it is not to be confined
in my tower cell—where they have
imprisoned me well over a
long year—to feel the spring sun on
my skin! What is it that these angry
men so fear that they treat me like
a criminal? They say it was
a sin to stand up for Charles
and for France. Yes, I carried sword
and shield and lance onto the teeming
battlefield, but I have never
been untruthful or concealed my
true intentions. They say I am
a sorceress, but that is only
an invention to protect them
from their own dark villainy, their
unmanly apprehensions
and disguised anxieties. They
are angry that I would not give
them satisfaction by saying
I was guilty or signing a
retraction. But I will not let
them harvest the bitter seeds of
fear they've sown. I am not afraid

because I am not alone. Saint
Margaret and Saint Catherine will
never desert me. They will keep their
promise: No one can hurt me.

FIRE

I will I will I will my darling
I will I will I will
I thrill I thrill I thrill my darling
I thrill I thrill I thrill
I burn I burn I burn my darling
I burn I burn I burn
I yearn I yearn I yearn my darling
yea I a rn

❧ SAINT CATHERINE ❧

Barbers and bakers approach me in prayer,
and those who know their philosophy,
and lawyers and young girls with long, unbound hair
and wheelwrights and scribes, too, supplicate me,
and millers and preachers and potters feel free
to beg and beseech me. I do what I can,
but I am not now what I once used to be.
Saints are only human.

I would also like to make you aware
I converted to true Christianity
hundreds of pagans. I once had a flare
for debate, religion, theology,
was renowned for the skill of my oratory.
Oh, yes, I was quite the sesquipedalian.
But all that is gone. I'm exhausted. You see,
saints are only human.

There once was a princess with long, flowing hair,
lovely, and also quite scholarly.
But she was beheaded—a messy affair—
for refusing to take vows of matrimony.
In case you were wond'ring, that princess was me.
He was a repulsive, ridiculous man!

If I'm slightly resentful, I think you'll agree,
saints are only human.

About this young Joan I've some sympathy,
but if I forgot her, reneged on the plan,
she'll learn the hard way: There's no guarantee.

Saints are only human.

JOAN

The journey to Chinon—eleven
days and nights—was long and hard. I
had always to be on my guard,
for not only was I in the
company of men who were not
of my blood, but the rivers were
high, in spring flood, and we traveled
through countryside the English
controlled. But I was comforted,
consoled, by the voices of my
saints. My male escorts showed constraint
and never once approached me with
impure innuendos or dis-
honorable intentions. My
accusers often mention this
as proof that I'm a witch, a wicked
necromancer. They say the only
way they can explain why healthy
men remained aloof to what is
vital to their sex was I had
practiced conjuring to produce
unnatural effects. They insist
that I had cast a spell; they insist
my voices come from Hell. They insist

I am a zealot of the black
demonic arts. They insist on
evil everywhere but in the
darkness of their hearts.

AT night, Jeanne slept beside Jean de Metz and myself, fully dressed and armed. I was young then; nevertheless I never felt towards her any desire: I should never have dared to molest her, because of the great goodness which I saw in her.

Bertrand de Poulengey, squire
Trial of Nullification

LUST

I was a snake
that would not strike,
a fawning tiger,
a blunted pike,
confused and
undirected.

I was hunger,
agitated,
always wanting,
never sated,
asking
but neglected.

A fire
unlit,
ale
not drunk,
a ripened bud
that grew
then shrunk,
a belfry unerected.

She was ice.
She was flame.
She was goodness.
She was my shame,
iniquity
reflected.

JOAN

Before we set out on our expedition,
I made another change. It is
the accepted tradition for
young women to arrange their hair
in long and flowing tresses. This
well-established custom expresses
they are of age and available
for marriage, and is a subtle
declaration to the opposite
sex. But I have never felt compelled
to do what everyone expects.
I took up a pair of shears. My
hair is now an easy length, cut
just below my ears.

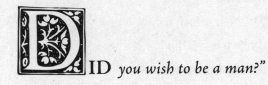

"**D**ID *you wish to be a man?*"

Trial of Condemnation

HER HAIR

I was
a flag,
a waving
splendor;
I was
a sign
to each
contender,
as full
of hope
as morning.

I am a wonder. I am ease.
I'm an avowal: I do what I
please. A fearless day aborning.

I was
encour-
agement.
I was
allure.
I was
a melody
flowing,

pure,
appealing, and
adorning.

I am a helmet on a strange head.
I am a word that won't be said,
 a triumph, and a warning.

JOAN

From the town of Fierbois, I relayed
my intention to see the dauphin,
a single day's ride from where he
held court. My saints had supported
our long expedition, and while
we awaited the dauphin's permission
to enter Chinon, I rested
and prayed, giving thanks to my voices
that we'd not been delayed by the
English or outlaws the war had
created. I was impatient
but also elated, for soon
I would kneel before the chosen
king of France, nevermore to tend
my father's bleating sheep nor weed
the tender plants in my mother's
kitchen plot. I welcomed who I
was and left behind who I was
not. The chapel at Fierbois was built
of stone and wood, and I
attended Mass there as often as
I could, finding happiness and
strength as I knelt before its altar.

Never once did I falter or doubt
I would succeed. My saints—they would
sustain me and give me everything
I need.

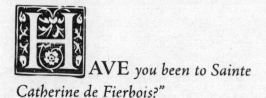"**H**AVE *you been to Sainte Catherine de Fierbois?*"

Joan: *"Yes and I heard there three Masses in one day."*

Trial of Condemnation

THE ALTAR AT
SAINTE CATHERINE DE FIERBOIS

For hundreds of years, I've attended prayers of peasants and nobility, their earthly cares, their hopes, their needs, their gravest sins, so many secrets that it begins to encumber me. Stained with salt of countless tears for hundreds of years, I'm burdened by the solemn pleas, the quivering voices, the bruisèd knees of desperate, suffering penitents. They have repeated the same sentiments, intoned the same vows, or so it appears, for hundreds of years. The secrets I know, I keep interred; unforgivable sin and damning word are buried with other mysteries, swords left by knights to calm and please a vengeful god who saw their sins. Oh, the secrets I know are crushing me. But she was different from the rest. She asked for nothing, no fervent request. I was both purified and awed when, in emptiness, she offered herself to God and, baptized in her ecstasy, I surrendered and let go of the secrets I know.

JOAN

To lift the siege at Orléans
was my initial charge. Henry
had the town surrounded, his army
large and well-supplied. The citizens
were starving but would not be
occupied by an invading foreign
power and so were forced to cower
in their homes like sparrows in a
storm when English arrows rained,
unable to maintain their lives
without the fear of death. The English
only had to hold their breath for
the town to fall. Saint Margaret and
Saint Catherine said that Orléans
must not be lost. I had to lift
the siege, whatever it might cost.
But first I had to gain the dauphin's
confidence. For that I would rely
upon my holy saints and my
own intelligence. Word of our
mission traveled faster than we.
News had spread of the prophecy,
and when we rode into Chinon,
the narrow streets were crowded. I,

Joan, a peasant, a girl, was being
celebrated, lauded by the
townsfolk who were shouting, reaching
out to touch my arm or leg and
begging me to deliver France from
its English enemies. Was it so
wrong of me to feel pleased to
hear them calling out "The Maid!" as
our small cavalcade made its way
through the throng? Wrong of me to take
pride in how far I had come? Sinful
to take pleasure in the sweet hum of
hope that filled the air? Everywhere
I looked—faces smiling, laughing,
cheering! Cheering in a time of
misery and war! I loved these
people, the faithful poor. But we were
nearing the castle, the residence
of Charles, the gentle dauphin
and rightful king. I had never
seen anything so majestic
or so grand. Its towers and its
battlements fanned out on the very
top of the hill that overlooked

the town, like a protective helmet
or a shining, royal crown. My
voices whispered I would soon stand
on its parqueted and polished floors;
but they did not warn me of the
darkness lurking in its corridors.

FTER *dinner, I went to the King, who was at the Castle. When I went to the room where he was I recognized him among many others by the counsel of my Voice, which revealed him to me. I told him I wished to go and make war on the English.*

Joan
Trial of Condemnation

THE CASTLE AT CHINON

Only

a child trapped

in the thrall of palace

rooms that wind and sprawl—each

hung with gaudy tapestries whose func-
tion is to warm and please the noble folk
when winter's squall explodes against the
tower wall and muffles the pathetic call of
courtiers begging on their knees—only a
child could not attend the pleading wail,
the pain, the misery, the pall, that radiate
and rise from these: the blood spills and
the treacheries that fester in these lurid
halls—only a child. Where kings reside,
the sleeping dust on gilded frames knows
not to trust anything a king might say. A
promise that he makes today, though
he proclaims it with robust sincerity, is
worthless. Just and wise men know that
greed and lust, deceit and treason, often
play where kings reside a game in which
the drag and thrust of power that is won
and lost leaves innocence to die, decay. It
is a virtue to betray where kings reside.

JOAN

When finally I saw Charles—
after two days of waiting,
worrying, wondering, anticipating—
they tried to deceive me. His male
advisors did not believe me
and so they put him in disguise
and introduced another as
he. The look on their faces! The shock
and surprise when they saw that I
was not so easily misled.
How their jaws dropped when I smiled
and said, "But this man is false, a
giddy pretender." And in the
splendor of the court went directly
to Charles and gave him my knee.
My voices told me it was he. I
then described for him my vision,
my saints, my voices, and my mission
to lift the siege at Orléans.
We went into a private room,
and there in the solemn and imposing
gloom, I gave my king a sign that

everything I'd said was true. I
told him something that only he
knew—the content of his secret prayers.

WAS *at the Castle of the town of Chinon when Jeanne arrived there, and I saw her when she presented herself before the King's Majesty with great lowliness and simplicity; a poor little shepherdess! I heard her say these words: "Most noble Lord Dauphin, I am come and am sent to you from God to give succor to the kingdom and to you."*

Sieur de Gaucort
Trial of Nullification

CHARLES VII

What an embarrassment to me—
this peasant wench dressed in men's clothes!
To come before me! Royalty!
In tunic! Doublet! And in hose!

A reprehensible affront that goes
against all laws of propriety!
She says she is unschooled. It shows!
What an embarrassment to me!

To all the aristocracy!
She should be whipped! But then suppose . . .
suppose that her hyperbole—
this peasant wench dressed in men's clothes—

suppose she speaks the truth. A Christian knows
that God's work is a mystery;
she may well be the one He chose.
To come before me, royalty,

takes unusual bravery.
Can she defeat our English foes,
deliver France its victory,
in tunic, doublet, and in hose?

My noble courtiers oppose
her and her tale of prophecy.
Yet she was able to disclose
words I'd said in secrecy.
What an embarrassment!

JOAN

Before I could set upon my
mission to roust the English, save
Orléans, and lift the siege, Charles,
the dauphin, my king, and my liege,
accompanied me to Poitiers,
where the learnèd scholars of the
day convened to test and question
me. Their knowledge of theology
would tell the king with certainty
if my suit was false or true.
For three long weeks they put me through
a ceaseless and a silly trial.
Question after question, and all
the while Orléans was bleeding.
The proceedings of the trial
even called for rough and intimate
examinations to make sure
I was intact. I endured this
humiliation. If not, they
would have said that I had made a
pact with Hell. I know them well, these
men, always looking for the worst.
The world is cursed with them, but my
king needed their assurance, their

trust, their word that I was who I
said I was, and so with my
saints and my virginity, I
submitted and endured. I did
not let them see that I was
disquieted and bored. Instead, I sent
an urgent message to Fierbois,
asking for another sword, a
blade that I thought suited me very,
very well—a hero's sword from
long ago, the sword of Charles Martel.

SENT to seek for a sword which was in the Church of Sainte Catherine de Fierbois, behind the altar; it was found there at once; the sword was in the ground, and rusty; upon it were five crosses; I knew by my Voices where it was. . . . I wrote to the Priests of the place, that it might please them to let me have this sword, and they sent it to me. It was under the earth, not very deeply buried, behind the altar, so it seemed to me.

Joan
Trial of Condemnation

THE SWORD AT FIERBOIS

Asleep for
seven hundred
years, laid here to
rest by Charles
Martel. Then *she*
arrives
and inter-
feres. Sleep
for seven hun-
dred years has
not erased
the screams,
the fears of
all the souls
I've sent to
Hell. Asleep
for seven hun-
dred years, laid
here to rest by
Charles Martel.
He saved France
from the Saracen
some seven cen-
turies ago, a
time of war,
when daring
men saved France
from the Saracen, men like Martel. We two have been where no good man
should ever go. We saved France from the Saracen some seven centuries
ago. I've had my
fill of human
strife; I've had my
taste of human
blood. No more
the bow, the lance,

the knife. I've
had my fill. Of
human strife—
the battlefields
so ripe, so rife
with misery and
dung and mud?
I've had my fill
of human strife.
I've had my taste
of human blood.
Who told the
girl I rested here?
How could she
have known? A
saint? A sorcer-
ess? A seer? Who
told the girl I
rested here, forc-
ing me to reap-
pear, rise from
my bed of earth
and stone? Who
told the girl? I
rested here! How
could she have
known?

JOAN

I know that swords are necessary
things: Without them there can be no
war. But what they were invented
for is not a skill that I revere.
No matter how it may appear,
though I have ridden into fierce
and violent campaigns and have
suffered stinging losses and enjoyed
exalted gains that come with
any great hostility, neither
in the revenge of defeat nor
the madness of victory have
I used a sword to take another's
life. I've never made a widow
of an Englishman's wife, never
caused a soldier's blood to flow and
spill. I was born to lead and to
inspire, not to maim and kill.

These illusions and distracting
memories help to ease the pain
and fear of the burning present.
The sun, which I used to love, I
now lament, for he is now my

fiercest adversary. With every
second he climbs higher and brings
me closer to his functionary:
fire.

FIRE

I soar I soar I soar my darling
I soar I soar I soar
I will I will I will my darling
I will I will I will
I thrill I thrill I thrill my darling
I thrill I thrill I thrill
I burn I burn I burn my darling
I burn I burn I burn
I arn y I ea y rling
yea I a rn

JOAN

Time was squandered at Poitiers.
As day followed day followed day
followed day, the king was anguished,
in despair, as despondent as
a frightened hare caught in an English
trap. He was young and had no guide,
no recourse, no map to tell him
what to do. Each hour that passed brought
him closer to the day when Orléans
would capitulate. He was anxious,
moody, desperate. But finally
the decision came. The priests could
find in me "no blame." They assured
the king they could discern no harm.
And though it maddened and alarmed
his aides, he paid to have me fitted
with the hard accouterments
of war.

HE *King gave her a complete suit of armor and an entire military household.*

Louis de Contes
Trial of Nullification

THE ARMOR

I did my job;
I did my very best
to shield her from the pain of injury. But it was all in vain. She
would not rest until she had been captured and oppressed.
She'd always been her own worst enemy. But *I* did
my job. I did! My very best plate against her legs
and back and chest, my chain protecting neck and
wrist and knee. But it was all in vain. She would not
rest while Henry's English army still possessed
a single hectare of French land. Still, don't you
see, I did my job? I did my very best to slow
her down, but she could not be suppressed
by the weight of steel or by rationality.
My work was all in vain; she would not rest.
I did my job, but *she?* She was possessed by
some internal fire, consumed, obsessed. I *did* my job
and did my very best, yet my ambition was in vain.
She would not rest.

JOAN

Orléans was to be my test.
If I could lift the siege and
arrest the progress of the English
there, bait and defeat them the way
the hunter does a savage bear,
the king would know that I was not
a charlatan or fraud, that in
truth, I had been sent by God to
save France from its English enemies,
to chase them from our homeland and
to bring Henry to his knees. Orléans
had been surrounded for eight long
and trying months. Charles had tried
more than once to liberate the
town, but each time he'd been defeated.
His meager resources now depleted,
his enemies grew stronger, his
most accomplished knights no longer
able to break the might of the
filthy English scourge, or purge them
from their fortified positions.
I sent the English captains a
warning with grave admonitions

that unless they withdrew before
another morning's dew had fallen
on French soil, they would find themselves
in the turmoil of defeat. They
laughed and called me whore. I was just
a girl. No more than sixteen with
no experience of war and
no military training. They
must have thought me very entertaining.
That was their mistake. At daybreak
I led my army into Orléans,
unopposed and undetected.
The way the town greeted me, cheering
and calling for the Maid, reflected
the long and bloody price they'd paid,
their anguished months of suffering, their
awful desperation. I told
them to take heart. Their liberation
had arrived. They had survived in
order to be saved. How they wept
and laughed and cheered and waved while their
great relief and happiness drifted
on the air! And how my spirits

lifted with their steadfast faith in me.
Where are they now, those shining hours,
those brilliant days of victory?

VICTORY

I am a pail
that will not hold.
I am a fire
that soon burns cold,
the first half
of a story.

I am a bird
that won't be held,
a godhead's name
that's been misspelled.
Both truth
and allegory.

A paramour
who will not wake,
a round of bread
that will not bake.
A trickster's repertory.

I am a war cry,
bold and brash.

I am kindling.
I am ash,
 an evanescent glory.

JOAN

On the first morning of the fight
as light fell just after dawn, an
English arrow struck deep between
my neck and shoulder. The sight of
my own blood sickened me, but it
also made me bolder. Though I
was bleeding badly, I did not
leave the field of battle but
continued leading my brave men,
shouting we were not chattel of
the English but the liberators
of all France. "Advance!" I cried out
through the pain.

"Advance!"

"Advance!"

"Advance!"

THE *twenty-seventh of May, very early in the morning, we began the attack on the Boulevard of the bridge. Jeanne was there wounded by an arrow which penetrated half-a-foot between the neck and the shoulder; but she continued nonetheless to fight, taking no remedy for her wound.*

Jean, bastard of Orléans, count of Dunois
Trial of Nullification

THE ARROW

It
makes
no sense.
She should
have died. I saw
my mark and I
went deep. My gift
ignored. My joy denied.
It makes no sense. She
should have died. The pain she
seemed to brush aside: She was a
vow I could not keep. It makes no
sense. She should have died. I saw
my mark   and I
went   deep.

JOAN

Then as now I was guided by
my voices. All the choices I
made in the bloody days that followed
came from my hallowed saints, including
the constraints I put on my men
when the English gave up and departed.
Some thought me weak or tenderhearted,
for I had spoken to Henry's
captains, promising their safe retreat.

The English defeat had shown the
king that I was his protector
and salvation. My success was
irrefutable, a clear and
certain confirmation that faith
in me would lead him to triumphant
victory. I did not want to
stain this gift with needless butchery.
At the siege of Orléans, I
finished what I started. My
strategy was simple: We would
fight until we won. And in eight
short days, I, Joan, a peasant girl,
did what in eight long and crimson
months no clever man had done.

IT was said that Jeanne was as expert as possible in the art of ordering an army in battle, and that even a captain bred and instructed in war could not have shown more skill; at this the captains marveled exceedingly.

Maître Aignan Viole
Trial of Nullification

JOAN

We went on to be victorious
in other towns the English held.
Word spread; my forces swelled. Farmers
joined my army with nothing more
than spikes; some had only pitchforks,
some only wooden pikes. They asserted
as much chivalry as any
royal knight. In all, I had six
thousand men, each eager to be
led by me. We took Jargeau,
Meung-sur-Loire, and long bridged
Beaugency.

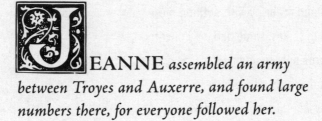 EANNE *assembled an army between Troyes and Auxerre, and found large numbers there, for everyone followed her.*

Gobert Thibaut, squire to the king of France
Trial of Nullification

THE PITCHFORK

I
used to
know the far-
mer's way, the
ups and
downs of his
routine. I spent
my time with
field. And hay
I used to know.
The farmer's
way is unim-
passioned. On
a lovely sum-
mer's day the
sky was blue,
the field was
green. I used
to know the
farmer's way,
the ups and
downs of
his routine.

Now
I know
the shock of
red; the farm
is only mem-
ory; the hay is
soaked with
blood that
shed. And
now I know
the shock of
red, stained
with an enemy
who bled and
died because
of me. Now I
know the
shock of red;
the farm is
only memory.

Why
did he
leave the field
and cow to
chase this
virgin from
Lorraine?
Abandoning
both hearth
and plow —
why did he
leave the field?
And how did
I become
what I am
now, a cham-
pion of pain?
Why did he
leave the field
and plow to
chase this
virgin from
Lorraine?

JOAN

I loved the military life,
though it was often rife with
peril, the men I fought with nearly
feral when their blood was up. I
shared their food. I shared their cup.
When they slept depleted on the
unforgiving ground, I lay there
too, surrounded by the sound of
soldiers in their dreams. The moan, the
muttered word, the restlessness, the
sigh, were as comforting to me
as any lullaby and proof I
was not mending seams or tilling
rocky land. Instead I was in
firm command of brave and fighting
men. The war is not yet over,
but I will not see those thrilling
days or know that happiness again.

FIRE

I roar I roar I roar my darling
I roar I roar I roar
I soar I soar I soar my darling
I soar I soar I soar
I will I will I will my darling
I will I will I will
I thrill I thrill I thrill my darling
I thrill I thrill I thrill
I bu b rn I n my ling
rn n I bu
I arn y I ea y rling
yea I a rn

JOAN

My saints were always there beside
me, to counsel, cheer, console, and
guide me. And they helped in other
ways: We were marching in the summer
haze toward the commune of Patay,
where English captains, bold and sly,
had set a snare, their men concealed
among the trees. With ready bows
and hungry swords they waited to
attack. But before this black plan
could be enacted and embraced,
a stag raced from a clearing.
Appearing from nowhere, large and wild,
he charged into the woods where the
Englishmen were hiding. I was,
as always, riding at the head
of my troops and saw frightened groups
of Henry's soldiers scatter, the
clatter of their swords as good a
warning as an alarm. They knew
the fatal harm the stag's sharp
antlers could impose. A clever
ambush was thus exposed. Four thousand
English died that day, the awful

price they had to pay for their flagrant
treachery, but their agonizing
loss was our tremendous victory.
Who but my saints would send that stag,
as sure a signal as a flag
alerting me to jeopardy?
I know this as surely as I
know my father's cattle graze
unshod: The stag was sent to me
by Heaven; the stag was sent to
me by God.

THINK *that Jeanne was sent by God, and that her behavior in war was a fact divine rather than human. Many reasons make me think so.*

Jean, bastard of Orléans, count of Dunois
Trial of Nullification

THE STAG

She says it was Heaven. I say it was Hell
that morning in the woodland glade
when unannounced and unafraid
I charged those soldiers. Who can tell?

Four thousand men died in that dell.
I can't forget the serenade
of dying screams, the acrid smell
of bitter blood beneath the blade

on the soft ground where they fell.
They'd gone to Mass, confessed and prayed,
and still transformed from man to shade,
the clash of swords their clanging knell.
She says it was Heaven. I say it was Hell.

JOAN

After victory at Orléans
and the Battle of Patay, the
king had confidence that I, and
I alone, could rescue France. My
voices said to take the king to
Reims, where he would at last be
consecrated by the holy
oil with which French kings must be
anointed. The men around him
were pointed in their discouragement
of this dangerous endeavor,
for we would ride through land that
Henry's soldiers held. They were clever,
these advisors, warning that the
English would never be expelled
if Charles were caught and in their
hands. But even as they spoke, Henry's
men were thriving on French lands,
growing fatter every day. In
this matter, I told Charles he
should have no fear. I was sent here
to protect him. Thanks to my saints,
the weaker counsel did not infect
him. In the budding month of June

we began our appointed journey:
the king, his court, my army, and
at the head of the procession,
me, mounted on my charger. He
was larger than other horses
and in possession of a wild
and fearless temperament. That we
belonged together was evident
from my first time on his back, me
commanding in my armor, him,
proud and shining black.

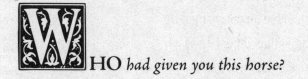 HO *had given you this horse?*

Joan: *"My King, or his people, from the King's money."*

Trial of Condemnation

THE WARHORSE

Not for me the slow life of the field and the plow
and the farm and the farmer's dull monotone
as he harvests and rakes while the sweat of his brow
drops to the soil like the seeds he has sown.

I was bred for the babel; I was bred for the how
and the why of the fight and the withering groan.
Not for me the slow life of the field and the plow
and the farm and the farmer's dull monotone.

I was bred for the knight and his bellicose vow
to enter the fray. Muscled loin, strong of bone,
firm of heart, wild of eye. Who would dare disavow
the bond of my breeding, the courage I've shown?

Not for me the slow life of the field and the plow.

And she was like me and so we were one.
We were the wind, untamed, unafraid
of the enemy's grit; we were fierce renegades,
unflagging, unyielding, until we had done

what we set out to do. There was none
who could check us; though she was a maid,

she was like me and so we were one
when we were the wind, untamed, unafraid.

Many a knight had been cowed and outdone
by my spirit, left broken, unseated, unmade.
But she understood. Unbridled blood runs
molten and wild, unrestrained, unsurveyed.

And she was like me and so we were one.

JOAN

The shuffling of the soldiers' feet
raised a tremendous cloud of dust
that could be seen from a great distance.
It gave the captains of the towns
the time to know if they should continue
their resistance or come to a
more peaceable decision. Would
they recognize their rightful king
and enjoy his supervision?
Or would they fight? One after another
they stepped out of English darkness
and came back to the French light.
Cravant, Bonny, Lavau, all welcomed
us, and Saint-Fargeau fell without
a fuss, not a single arrow
in the air. And so it was with
Coulanges, Brinon, Saint-Florentin,
Auxerre. I always rode ahead
to let them know the Maid was at
their door, foolish to oppose, at
their great peril to ignore. And

in the wind, the banner Charles
made for me—white, depicting
angels, and golden fleur-de-lis.

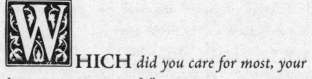

WHICH *did you care for most, your banner or your sword?"*

Joan: *"Better, forty times better, my banner than my sword."*

Trial of Condemnation

THE BANNER

Above her head the sparrows huddle in the trees. Above her
head they listen with increasing dread. The phantoms
of her enemies are wailing in the morning
breeze above her head. Above her head
I scream a terrifying prayer. Above her head,
a warning from the newly dead to not resist for who
would dare to fight the angels singing there above her head?

JOAN

Reims, too, was in English hands but,
before a sword had left its sheath,
it gave in to my demands. Not a
halberd thrown or a single word
of coarse debate. The residents
opened wide their city's gates as
the frightened English soldiers fled.
All of Reims bowed its head when Charles
rode through its cobbled streets. Word of
my military feats had also
reached their ears. I saw their suffering
faces wet with tears of unchecked joy
and raw relief. But to my eventual
sorrow and certain grief, in the
young king's retinue there were those
who, because I was not a man
but in men's clothes, thought I was a
blasphemer and a troublesome
disgrace. They resented my place
in the royal court and worked behind
my back to thwart my influence

with the king. I did nothing to
stop their gossip, their intimations,
or their tricks. My place was with my
king. I did not stoop to politics.
Instead, I attended to the
coronation. There is no apt
description nor sufficient explanation
for what occurred in the cathedral
there. The very air felt sanctified.
I was filled with joy and pride as
Charles VII, king of France, was
coronated and anointed.
I stood *beside* him–not behind.
And appointed in my finest
armor, I reminded myself
that I, the daughter of a lowly
farmer, had brought this holy day about.
I still can hear the people shout . . .

Or is that the throng in front of
me calling me a slut and witch,
their faces warped in anger, their
din a frenzied pitch?

FIRE

I'm near I'm near I'm near my darling
I'm near I'm near I'm near
I roar I roar I roar my darling
I roar I roar I roar
I soar I soar I soar my darling
I soar I soar I soar
I will I will I will my darling
I il l I will I w ll
thr I ill I thr my d rl ng
I thr I ri I

JOAN

But my king could save me still. If
he has the will, he could ransom
me. The price would be handsome, but
he could set me free. Everything
I did for France—he won't forget.
Charles is God's chosen king:
I know he'll save me yet.

CHARLES VII

What an embarrassment to me—
this peasant wench dressed in men's clothes!
To appear before me! Royalty!
In tunic! Doublet! And in hose!

A reprehensible affront that goes
against all laws of propriety!
She says she is unschooled. It shows!
What an embarrassment to me!

JOAN

There was so much more to do after
the victory at Reims. Henry
still held a large expanse of French
land, and Paris, too, was in his
grip. Though my voices did not tell
me to, with the approval and
companionship of my men and
the king, I set my sights on that
great city. There would be no mercy
and no solace, no pity for
the false French who there resisted,
whose loyalties had been so grossly
twisted that they would dare defy
me. I needed Charles to stand
beside me, but for seven long
weeks he reveled in his coronation
and stopped at every town that
welcomed him for drink and celebration.
By the time we reached the city
gates, our fates were set and firmly
sealed, for the English had prepared
themselves and concealed weapons and
ammunition around and on
the city walls—stones, crossbows,

cannonballs ready to be fired.
My men were eager and inspired,
their courage hot and high, but an
archer caught me in the thigh, and
the aide who held my banner also
fell, and with it our offense. My
army lost its confidence. When
I was carried from the field, Charles
ordered a withdrawal and my men
were forced to yield.

ID *you not say before Paris, 'Surrender this town by the order of Jesus'?"*

Joan: *"No, but I said, 'Surrender it to the King of France.'"*

Trial of Condemnation

THE CROSSBOW

Her
flesh was
tender, warm,
So firm and
soft. Like bread.

Her blood so rich and red. The pain I gave her muscled meat—her flesh!—was tender, warm, and sweet.

and sweet.

Her flesh was tender, warm, and sweet. Her blood so rich and red. She could not walk. She could not ride. I made sure of that. She challenged me and I replied, *You will not walk. You will not ride.* I struck and laid her flat. She could not walk.

She could not ride.
I made sure of that.
And still I did not
strike her heart,
though I had op-
portunity. I am a
master of my art,
and still I did not
strike her heart. I
don't know where

to turn to start to fathom my reluctancy. And still I did not strike her heart, though I had opportunity. Her flesh was tender, warm, and sweet. Her blood so rich. And red the pain I gave. Her muscled meat—her flesh!—was tender. Warm and sweet. Firm and soft, like bread. Her flesh was tender. Warm and sweet, her blood. So rich and red.

JOAN

The king seemed to retreat from me
after my defeat at Paris.
It was the ferrous tongues of my
detractors that caused this change in
his opinion. Among his minions
at the royal court, bad actors
undermined the king's support by
telling him my character and
comportment would taint his
reputation as a good and
Christian king. I was, they said, an
aberration. A girl who dressed
and acted like a man was a
sinful, monstrous thing he should no
longer tolerate. I'd served my
usefulness, they said. He should remain
aloof. They said I'd been abandoned
by my saints, and Paris was the
proof. My saints, too, which had always
come to me unbidden, remained
distant and silent, hidden unless
I called on them to ask for their
advice. I did this once or sometimes
twice a day. They never turned away

from me but they no longer charged
me with specific tasks as they
had at Orléans and Reims, and
I began to ask myself if
I'd fulfilled my duty to
my king and to my country, France.
But how could I return to
Domrémy, its drudging tasks and
dreary obligations? The military
life had its deprivations, but
it was what I loved and wanted.
I would not be shunted back to
the barn and field, not allow my
current life to be repealed by
the domestic rut I hated,
to be betrothed, wed and mated,
like all the girls I used to know.

A kind of fearful loneliness
began to germinate and grow.
I felt abandoned, almost ill,
and shaken and so I became
bolder still and started to take
risks I ought not to have taken.

At Compiègne, I rode out among
the English forces—their angry peasant
footmen, their knights on armored horses—
in a cloak of shining gold. I
told myself that once they behold
the Maid of Orléans, fierce and
gleaming in her splendor, they would,
like all the other towns, come to
their senses and surrender. But
the English there were not as
easily impressed as I had
thought. A common soldier grabbed the
cloak. He pulled me from my horse, and
I was captured, caught not only
by a footman who had his eye
on me, but also by my recklessness
and the sin of vanity. I
loved that cloak; it made me feel
invincible and like a royal
son. How confusing that I love
it still, though through it I have been
undone.

AD *not your Voices ever told you that you would be taken?"*

Joan: *"Yes, many times and nearly every day. And I asked of my Voices that, when I should be taken, I might die soon, without long suffering in prison: and they said to me: 'Be resigned to all—that it must be.' But they did not tell me the time; and if I had known it, I should not have gone. Often I asked to know the hour: they never told me."*

Trial of Condemnation

THE GOLD CLOAK

We were as splendid

as the noonday sun,

and in our glory would

blind our staring enemy.

But all stars fall when their

time to shine is done. Our fame

was known to everyone. Taken

with our own mythology, as bright

and splendid as the noonday sun, we

fought our battles. One by one by one,

singing, shouting, "Victory!" But all stars

fall. When their time to shine is done they

fade and disappear. None can escape that dull

and awful certainty, though once they shined as

splendid as the noonday sun. What we'd begun

ended. Now it's only history, like stars that fall when

their time to shine is done. She wasn't able to outrun her

fate. Each of us has a destiny as sure and splendid as the

noonday sun. But all stars fall when their time to shine is

d   o   n   e   .

JOAN

I was taken on the twenty-
third of May, and the next day they
brought me to Beaulieu les Fontaines.
But when, in July, I nearly
broke free, they improved their
weak security and removed me
to the tower at Beauvoir. It
was a foul place; the air was sour
but the windows lacked bars: My cell
was seven stories high. Was it my
intention, when I jumped, to enter
Paradise and die? Or did I
believe my blessèd saints would
teach me how to fly?

AVE you never done anything against their [her Voices'] command and will?"

Joan: *"All that I could and knew how to do I have done and accomplished to the best of my power. As to the matter of the fall [leap] at Beauvoir, I did it against their command; but I could not control myself. When my Voices saw my need, and that I neither knew how nor was able to control myself, they saved my life and kept me from killing myself."*

Trial of Condemnation

THE TOWER

In
another life,
I might have been
a crimson dress made
to inhibit and oppress, worn
by women, cut and sewn. Now my
skin is mortared stone made by men for
war and strife. In another life
she might have been a man,
no more an anomaly than
any other natural man. Not
a danger. Not a threat. Then
she and I would not have met.
She might have been a farmer's wife in another life.

JOAN

I still don't understand why I
did not die the afternoon I
leapt. Do my saints think this a better
way? To be kept like a beast in
a darkened cell? To never see
the light of day? To be consumed
by smoke and choking fire? Did I
not do well in what they asked of
me? In what way did I offend?
Does my death require something that
I cannot comprehend? Or might
Saint Margaret save me still? The sun
is nearly at its peak, but she
has asked me to have faith. And so
I will.

❧ SAINT MARGARET ❧

Faith isn't for the faint of heart.
Both courage and naïveté
are required. To grasp its art,
you must look the other way
when all the omens seem to say
you will not get what you desire,
so, though it may be a cliché,
I put my faith in fire.

Flames are devoted. Once they start
their urgent work—some call it play—
you may depend, they won't depart
until they've kept their word. Their way
is not to waver; they obey
a law more natural. As they grow higher
they will not falter or betray.
So put your faith in fire.

Fire will scorch and singe and smart;
she cannot keep its pain at bay.
It will destroy her, then depart,
leaving ashes, cold and gray.
Though she may beg and plead and pray,

make promises, repent, conspire,
her time has come. It's judgment day.
She'll put her faith in fire.

If I said, *Have faith* that day,
and if *In what?* she had inquired,
I would have told her straightaway,

In fire, my dear, in fire.

JOAN

From Beauvoir they moved me to Rouen,
where a bishop, Pierre Cauchon, was
the master of my trial. Even
now I see the backwards smile
that really was no smile at all.
He asked me to recall my youth,
which was unsettling for me. They
used my memory of the ancient
Fairy Tree to twist the truth and
say I was a young disciple
of the Fiend, the Evil One. Even
childhood's innocence can be knotted,
twisted, stretched, and spun if the spiders
are clever. When they were done, they'd
transformed those guiltless days into
debauched, unholy fun. Their minds
were sharp and coiled, like serpents
hiding in a maze. Such are evil
men, and their deceitful, bitter
ways. I'm glad my mother cannot
see me tied here to this stake. I
was her eldest daughter; it would
cause her heart to break.

THE STAKE

I am her best
a n d   o n l y
friend, her stal-
wart intimate.
On me she's
l e a r n e d   s h e
can depend. I
am her best
a n d   o n l y
friend. We'll
be upright to
the end. She
doesn't love
me, but I am
her best and
only friend,
her stalwart
intimate. We
stand together,
she and I. I'll
never let her
go. Until the
flames burn hot
and high we'll
stand together,
she and I. Let
our ashes tes-
tify, we stood
together. She
and I! I'll nev-
er let her
go!

JOAN

Cauchon was French but was a
henchman for the English, whose most
fervent wish was to prove the Maid
of Orléans the Devil's implement
and full of devilish tricks. His
loyalty was not to justice
but to the god of politics.

BISHOP PIERRE CAUCHON

I am a man of God, a simple *man*
of faith whose solemn duty is to *know*
with certainty, without the slightest *doubt*,
the great divide between wrong and *right*,
between good and evil, between false and *true*.
As a man of God, I have vowed to be always just
    and *fair*,

so never let it be said that I was not *fair*
in my dealings with this "maid," for as a man of
    God, a simple *man*
of faith who speaks the word of God, I know
    His *true*
and holy wishes. I know this just as surely as
    I *know*
that as a man ordained by God, it is my *right*
to judge this girl. There can be no *doubt*

about my God-given authority, no *doubt*
about my sacred mission to be just and *fair*,
no doubt that my intentions are always pure and
    my judgment always *right*,
for I am a man, a simple, pious, holy *man*

of faith and learning, a man of God who *knows*
in his soul and in the souls of all men what is
    false and just and right and *true*.

As a simple, holy man of faith and God, I know
    Henry is the *true*
king, and whosoever should question this truth
    or *doubt*
me is a blasphemer and a heretic and should be
    burned to purify his soul! *Know*
that he is the worshiper of Lucifer! An enemy of
    God's *fair*
and holy wishes! An agent of the Devil! I know
    this as a holy *man*
of simple faith, a fair and pious man of God who
    knows what is *right*

and what is wrong and what is just and what is
    true. It is my sacred task to set a*right*
whatever is abomination, false, sinful, unholy,
    unnatural, and un*true*.
It is a grave and sacred responsibility, though as a
    simple *man*

of holy faith, a pious man of God, I do not *doubt*
or question. And that is *fair*
and good and just and right. And I *know*

that everything I *know*
is *right*
and *fair*
and *true*.
I have no *doubt*.
I am a man of God, a holy, pious, faithful *man*.

Know this: That girl is an enemy to everything
    that's *right*
and holy and pious and sacred and *fair* and just
    and *true*!
How can you *doubt* me? She dresses like a *man*!

JOAN

For five long months they asked question
after question, and always the
same. In their hearts? Deception. In
their eyes? Revenge and blame.

"Why won't you wear
a woman's dress?"

"Do you wish to be a man?"

"Confess!"

"You are the Devil's tool! Renounce his wicked plan!"

"Don't you think that your comportment is a sin against your God?"

"Confess!"

"You are a charlatan!"

"Confess!"

"You are a fraud!"

But I made no such confession.
It seems to me my only real
transgression was to invade and
triumph in the sacred land of
men; a woman in their landscape
was a repugnant, mortal sin,
unless she was a loving wife
or kneeling nun or knowing
prostitute. They would have hated
me far less if I had been a
girl of ill repute instead of
what I was and who I am: a
girl who dared to live the life of
a brave and honest man.

FIRE

I'm here I'm here I'm here my darling

HE was taken to execution, with great anger, by the English soldiers. . . . She began to weep and call upon "Jesus." Then I went away, having so great compassion that I could not witness her death.

Brother Pierre Migier
Trial of Nullification

JOAN

I am come to the end. My saints
will not save me. I surrender
to the fire that craves me. Let him
finally take and ravage the Virgin
from Lorraine. The savage thrust, the
burning kiss, the penetrating
pain will be my ecstasy in
knowing I was true; there is nothing
I have done that I would alter
or undo. The lightning pain belongs
to me, is mine and mine alone.
I was the Maid of Orléans.
I was a girl called Joan.

✳ EPILOGUE ✳

...e glare of the sun. Sun.

Or a Holy One? (But some say it was on.

...ument that can't be won. Yet all agree she burned

...e blinding glare of the sun, alone in a circle of sacred lig

...d light. **Some say she walked in the glare of the sun.** Some sa

...the sun. **Some say a circle of sacred light. A mad girl?** Or a Holy

mad girl? **Or a Holy One? (But some say it was only the** glare of th

s only the **glare of the sun.) An argument that can't** be won. Yet al

that can't **be won. Yet all agree she burned too bright,** lost in the

o bright, **lost in the blinding glare of the sun,** alone in a circle c

he sun, **alone in a circle of sacred light.** Some say she walke

of the sun. Some say a circle of sacred light. A mad gir'

't some say it was only the glare of the sun.) Ar

Yet all agree she burned too bright '

...le of sacred li

AUTHOR'S NOTE

In 1429, two years before Joan of Arc was executed, Christine de Pizan, the esteemed poet at the court of Charles VI, wrote her last great epic, *Le ditié de Jehanne d'Arc*. This poem, *The Song of Joan of Arc*, is the only popular literature written about Joan in her lifetime. How cool would it be, I thought, if *my* Joan were to speak in the same form that Christine de Pizan used six hundred years ago in her sixty-one-stanza panegyric? *Very cool, right?*

Only, it wasn't.

Joan turned out to be as stubborn in the imagination as she was in real life. For months, I tried to get her to tell her story in Pizan's eight-line stanzas. And for months, she resisted. And so, as often happens, I had to put my very cool idea aside. In *Voices*, Joan now speaks in what might be described as a kind of toned-down spoken word.

But all was not lost. That one cool, but failed, experiment led to another. What if the other voices in the book spoke in the poetic forms that were popular during Joan's lifetime? Some of these forms—villanelles and sestinas, for example—are still very much in use by poets writing today. Others, like the ballade (not to be confused with the ballad), are much less popular.

For the sake of variety, I've included forms that were developed a bit later than Joan's lifetime, but many are those she herself might have heard, though, of course, in their original French. Adhering to the rules of these ancient verses became my way of honoring Joan, and it brought me closer to her and the people and time in which she lived. I hope they did the same for you.

Still, something vital was missing. But what? And then it hit me. In addition to the voice of the Joan I was imagining, I needed to give the real Joan and her associates the opportunity to speak for themselves. Fortunately, there was a way to do just that through the Trial of Condemnation and the Trial of Nullification.

As for the poems, the rules for each—governing such things as length, syllabic structure, and rhyme scheme—can be found easily enough online or by consulting, as I did every single day, Miller Williams's excellent *Patterns of Poetry: An Encyclopedia of Forms*. Poems not listed—"The Candle," for instance, or "Silence"—are, with one or two exceptions, patterns I copied from the songs of the troubadours. While I did not intentionally weave errors into the poems, I cannot say they are without flaws when it comes to the guidelines that define them.

BALLADE

* ✦ Saint Michael
* ✦ Saint Catherine
* ✦ Saint Margaret

RONDEAU

* The Castle at Chinon

RONDEAU REDOUBLÉ

* Charles VII

RONDEL

* The Cattle
* The Stag
* The Warhorse

RONDELET

* The Road to Vaucouleurs
* The Banner

SESTINA

* Isabelle
* Jacques d'Arc
* Robert de Baudricourt
* Bishop Pierre Cauchon

SHORT RONDEL

TRIOLET

VILLANELLE

ACKNOWLEDGMENTS

I would be a heartless cad indeed if I failed to mentioned the beautiful work of Sharismar Rodriguez, this book's designer. Her perseverance in dealing with an author who is a graphic nincompoop went far beyond what a human should have to endure. Any praises *Voices* receives is due in part to her skill, her patience, and her persistence.

Don't miss David Elliott's masterful fairy-tale retelling in verse!

1

CHANGE

AND this is the forest
With its primeval trees
And their taciturn trunks
And their hungering roots
Like curious tongues
That kiss the hard stones
And lap the warm rain
And speak to the earth
In the language of trees

And here are the limbs
Their itinerant twigs
The finely veined leaves
That are unblinking eyes
And the eyes watch the wolf
And the eyes watch the bear
And the eyes watch the back
Of the ravening boar
That runs wild through the forest
And when the wind howls
The eyes tumble down
And leave the trees blind

Behold the rough bark
With its numberless ears
That cling to the tree
And hear the birth pangs
Of the fox and the deer
And the growl of the cat
And the break of the branch
And the flight of the stag
And the screech of the owl
And the flap of its wing
And the cry of the hare
And the rip of soft flesh
And the silence of blood

AND this is the river

That runs through the forest

And the river's a rope

That cannot be tied

And the river's a secret

That cannot be told

And the river's a riddle

That cannot be guessed

And the river's a snake

Ever shedding its skin

And the river's a bow

On the strings of the earth

And the river's a mouth

That devours the sun

And the river's a throat

That swallows the moon

And the river's a song

That sings to itself

In the ancient and sibilant

Language of rivers

AND this is the cottage
That's built near the river
Its timbers are aching
Its floorboards are cracking
And creaking they're quaking
From so many boots
Stomping in stamping out
Eight pairs of boots
Stomping in stamping out
So many boots
Stomping in stamping out
Day after day after day after day
And the hearth burns too hot
And the thatch whispers *Stop*
And the footsteps are heavy
And the joists beg for mercy
But the heels have no pity
And the boots they keep coming
Eight pairs of boots
Stomping in stamping out
Day after day after day after day

ΛND here are the boys
Who live in the cottage
The eldest is Jack
And the next one is Jack
And the third one's called Jack
And the fourth's known as Jack
And the fifth says he's Jack
And they call the sixth Jack
But the seventh's not Jack
The seventh is Robyn
And this is his story

ROBYN

They called me Robyn. How did they know from
      the very start
that the murmuring beat of my infant heart
would not conform to the rhythms of my brothers'?
One no different from the other,
and insensible to the smart

sting of thorns on the rocky ground. Each of us,
      it seems, has his part
to play; theirs is earthbound, like our father's,
      their feet planted in the dirt.
But I love the sky, its incandescence, its infinity,
      its colors.
And they called me Robyn.

The naming of children is a fine and subtle art.
Parents must consider everything the name imparts.
Was it merely accident or the instinct of a mother
that mine hints at altitude and air, flight and feather?
Whether luck or Fate—Fortune's sly, unyielding
      counterpart—
they called me Robyn.

A̲N̲D̲ here is the man
Who lives in the cottage
That's built near the river
That runs through the forest
He calls himself Jack

And here is Jack's axe
With its bright-sharpened tongue
And its bright-sharpened will
And its head-banging anger
Its terrible temper
Its loathing of rest

And this is Jack's saw
With its sharp crooked teeth
And its lunatic grin
And its sickening song
And insatiable greed
And its obsessive need

        To go forth
and come back
        To go forth
and come back
        To go forth
and come back
        To go forth
and come back

AND day after day after day after day

Jack swings the sharp axe

And pulls the sharp saw

And curls the tongues

And tramples the eyes

And deafens the ears

And brings the trees down

He wants to know why

He has seven sons

When night after night after night after night

He falls on his knees

And clasps the scarred hands

That hold the dark beads

And bows the big head

That holds the dark eyes

And shuts out the noise

Of his sons in their sleep

And prays for a daughter

JACK

I do not ask for much or often,
but give me a daughter to soften
the keenly tapered edge of our lives.
Like an assassin, each day arrives,
shining, silent with his best-loved knives,
impatient to cut us down, impale,
overpower us as we travail.
It's the blighted fate of men like me
to wrestle with the despondency
yoked to their crippling poverty.
I need to hear a daughter's laughter,
see a daughter's gentle smile after
a long day's labor with seven boys—
the sweating, the hunger, and the noise.
Grant me the tender pleasures, the joys
that only a daughter can impart
to a father's troubled, loving heart.
Do this and I'll never ask again.
Amen. Amen. Amen. And amen.

AND this is Jack's wife
Let's call her Jane
Jane is a marshal
Her hands are her armies
Her fingers the soldiers
That follow Jane's orders
To break the hard earth
And plant the hard seeds
And pull the sharp weeds
And bake the coarse bread
And spin the fine thread
And weave the rough cloth
And mend the torn smocks
And the eight pairs of socks
Of her husband and sons

And when the night comes
And her husband is sleeping
And the Seven are sleeping
And the red cow is sleeping
And the horned goat is sleeping
And the fat hen is sleeping
And the kitten is sleeping

And all the world's sleeping
Jane lies awake

And dreams of a daughter

JANE

My boys and their father, they work hard
bringing down the trees, hands bruised and scarred
when a knot may cause the saw to slip.
But at least they have companionship.
There are days that loneliness will grip
and knead me, as if I were but dough.
But if I had a daughter, then . . . oh,
a girl to talk to! Someone like me,
a girl to ease the monotony
of this thrusting masculinity
that each day I am a witness to—
the constant fights to determine who
is strongest, their manners rude and coarse.
I could admonish them till I'm hoarse,
but they're men, and strangers to remorse.
I love my boys, but I cannot breathe.
Beneath this bridled calm, I seethe.
Some days I wish I could disappear.
I need a girl, a daughter with me here.

AND there's hair in the milk
And a smell in the cheese
And a snake in Jack's boot
And worms in the fruit
And a hole in Jane's pail
And the rye starts to fail
Mold grows on the bread
And the kitten is dead
And there's spot on the wheat
And rot in the goat
And bloat in the cow
And the thatch has turned black
And the axe bounces back
There are too many Jacks
There are too many Jacks
There are too many Jacks
There are too many Jacks